R0202486825

10/2021

AD570L

☑ **W9-AYO-571**

Twinkle
and the
Fairy Flower Garden

by Katharine Holabird · illustrated by Sarah Warburton

Ready-to-Read

Simon Spotlight

New York London Toronto Sydney New Delhi

SIMON SPOTLIGHT
An imprint of Simon & Schuster Children's Publishing Division
1230 Avenue of the Americas, New York, New York 10020
This Simon Spotlight edition July 2021
For information about special discounts for bulk purchases, please contact Simon & Schuster Special Sales at 1-866-506-1949 or business@simonandschuster.com.
Manufactured in the United States of America 0521 LAK
10 9 8 7 6 5 4 3 2 1
Library of Congress Cataloging-in-Publication Data
Names: Holabird, Katharine, author. | Warburton, Sarah, illustrator.
Title: Twinkle and the fairy flower garden / by Katharine Holabird ; illustrated by Sarah Warburton.
Description: Simon Spotlight edition. | New York : Simon Spotlight, 2021. | Series: Twinkle | Audience: Ages 5–7. | Summary: Twinkle and her classmates are planting a garden, but unlike everyone else's flowers, Twinkle's are not growing—until she realizes her seeds require special encouragement.
Identifiers: LCCN 2020036063 | ISBN 9781534486263 (paperback) | ISBN 9781534486270 (hardcover) | ISBN 9781534486287 (ebook)
Subjects: CYAC: Fairies—Fiction. | Gardening—Fiction. | Friendship—Fiction.
Classification: LCC PZ7.H689 Twje 2021 | DDC [E]—dc23
LC record available at https://lccn.loc.gov/2020036063

Twinkle and her friends
Lulu and Pippa were very excited.
Their teacher, Miss Flutterbee,
had a special surprise for all the
little fairies in her class.

"I know how much you all
love plants and flowers,"
Miss Flutterbee said.
"So we are going to plant
a lovely garden at
The Fairy School of Magic and Music!
You will each get your own seeds
to plant."

The sounds of giggles, cheers,
and fluttering fairy wings
filled the room.
Twinkle was so excited,
her wings glowed bright pink.
She had always wanted
to plant flowers!

"We can sing fairy songs
as we garden together!"
Twinkle told Lulu and Pippa.

"We can use acorn tops
as flower baskets!"
Pippa said.

"We can make flower crowns
for our hair!" said Lulu.

"We are going to have
so much fun!"
Twinkle said.
"It will be better than
sparkles and glitter and
sprinkles combined!"

The next day the class met
in the schoolyard.
Each fairy got a set of tools,
a sparkly watering can,
and frilly gardening gloves.

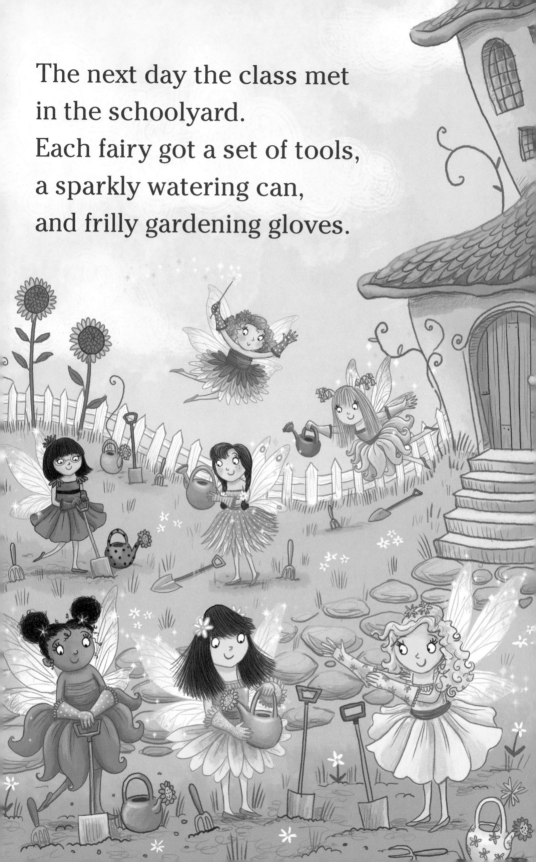

"My gloves are pink!"
Twinkle said.
"I love them so much."
Her wings glowed brighter
than ever!

Miss Flutterbee gave
each fairy a packet of seeds
and a plot of land to garden.
"Oooh, I have rose seeds!"
Lulu said.
"And I have bluebell seeds!"
Pippa said.

"I have special seeds!"
Twinkle said.
Then she frowned.
"What are special seeds?"
she asked Miss Flutterbee.

"It is a surprise!"
Miss Flutterbee said.
Twinkle did not want
a surprise. She wanted
pretty pink flowers!

It was time for the fairies
to find their garden plots.
"Here is mine!"
Lulu said.
"And mine is next to yours!"
Pippa said happily.

Twinkle was still
looking for her plot.
It was on the other side
of the garden!
"Mine is over here,"
Twinkle said.

Lulu and Pippa were too
far away to hear Twinkle.
Her wings glowed blue
with sadness.

"Fairies, it is time to
plant your seeds,"
Miss Flutterbee said.
Twinkle tried to remember
what she had learned in class.
First she dug little holes
in the soil.

She dropped a seed
into each hole.
She put soil on top.

Then she used her purple
watering can to sprinkle
water on the soil.

Twinkle looked over at
Pippa and Lulu, who were
singing as they planted.
"They look like they are
having so much fun,"
Twinkle said with a sigh.
"I wish I could be with them."

Then Miss Flutterbee said,
"Well done, fairies!
Now use a little magic to help
the seeds grow faster."
Twinkle waved her wand
and cast a spell,
"Fiddle-dee-gardens,
blossoms, and trees.
Grow peachy-pink flowers
as quick as you please!"

The next day the fairies
all raced back to see the garden.
Twinkle was so excited
to see what had grown
from her special seeds.

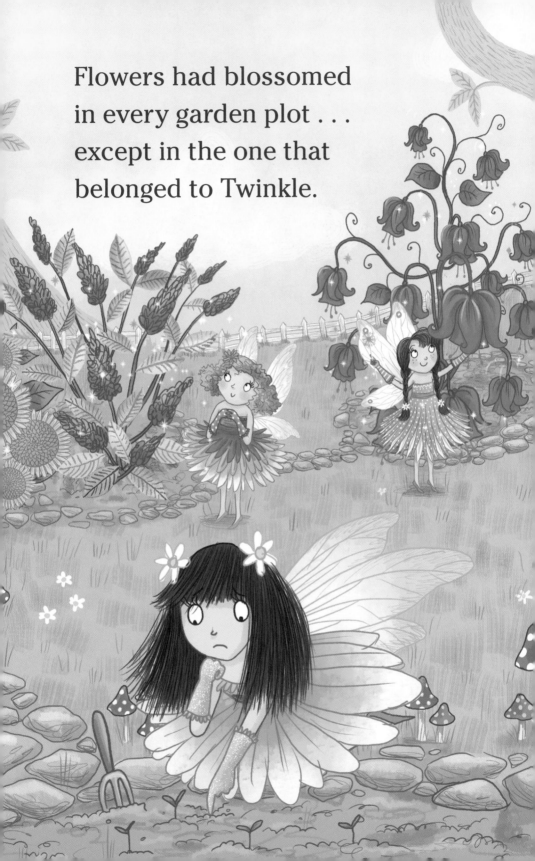

Flowers had blossomed
in every garden plot . . .
except in the one that
belonged to Twinkle.

"Sorry, Twinks,"
Lulu said.
"I am sure your seeds will
grow into flowers soon,"
said Pippa.

"Perhaps your special seeds
need a special spell?"
Miss Flutterbee hinted.

Twinkle gasped.
She had used a spell for
flower seeds.
"Maybe my seeds are not
like the other flower seeds,"
Twinkle realized.

Twinkle waved her wand
and tried a spell that would
help all kinds of plants grow.
"Oodles of fairy dust,
and doodles of glee.
May my seeds be what
they are meant to be!"

Now Twinkle had to wait.
"It is not easy to wait for
things to grow,"
Twinkle told Pippa and Lulu.
"Let's make flower crowns,"
Pippa said.
"I do not have flowers,"
Twinkle said sadly.

"We will share!" Lulu said.
"That is what friends do."
Together the three fairies
made beautiful bluebell and
rose crowns.

The next day Twinkle raced
to the garden to see if her
special spell had worked.
"Wowee!" Twinkle squealed.
The special seeds had grown
into strawberry plants with
tiny flowers and big red berries.

"I love strawberries!"
Twinkle cheered.
Miss Flutterbee told Twinkle
it was safe to eat the berries.
Twinkle filled an acorn top with
berries and shared them with
Lulu and Pippa.

"These are the best berries
I have ever had!" said Lulu.
"Yum!" said Pippa.
Twinkle smiled.
"I guess those seeds were
special after all!" she said.
"Thank you, Miss Flutterbee!"